To River
Love Gran & Gramp
December, 2022

First published 2013 Parragon Books, Ltd.

Copyright © 2018 Cottage Door Press, LLC
5005 Newport Drive, Rolling Meadows, Illinois 60008
All Rights Reserved

Written by Clement C. Moore
Illustrated by Henry Fisher

ISBN: 978-1-68052-456-7

Parragon Books is an imprint
of Cottage Door Press, LLC.
Parragon Books® and the Parragon® logo are
registered trademarks of Cottage Door Press, LLC.

The Night Before Christmas

By Clement C. Moore

Illustrated by Henry Fisher

PaRragon.

'Twas the night before Christmas,
when all through the house
Not a creature was stirring,
not even a mouse.

The stockings were hung
by the chimney with care,
In hopes that St. Nicholas
soon would be there.

The children were nestled all snug in their beds,
While visions of sugarplums danced in their heads.

And Mama in her kerchief, and I in my cap,
Had just settled down for a long winter's nap.
When out on the lawn there arose such a clatter,
I sprang from my bed to see what was the matter.

Away to the window I flew like a flash,
Tore open the shutters and threw up the sash.
The moon on the breast of the new-fallen snow
Gave luster of midday to objects below,
When, what to my wondering eyes should appear,
But a miniature sleigh and eight tiny reindeer.

With a little old driver so lively and quick,
I knew in a moment it must be St. Nick.

More rapid than eagles
his coursers they came,
And he whistled and shouted
and called them by name;

"Now Dasher! Now Dancer! Now Prancer and Vixen!
On Comet! On Cupid! On Donner and Blitzen!

"To the top of the porch! To the top of the wall!
Now dash away! Dash away! Dash away all!"

As dry leaves that before the wild hurricane fly,
When they meet with an obstacle, mount to the sky,
So up to the housetop the coursers they flew,

With a sleigh full of toys and St. Nicholas, too.
And then, in a twinkling, I heard on the roof
The prancing and pawing of each little hoof.

As I drew in my head, and was turning around,
Down the chimney St. Nicholas came with a bound.

He was dressed all in fur,
from his head to his foot,
And his clothes were all tarnished
with ashes and soot.
A bundle of toys he had flung on his back,
And he looked like a pedlar
just opening his pack.

His eyes—how they twinkled!
His dimples—how merry!
His cheeks were like roses, his nose like a cherry!
His droll little mouth was drawn up like a bow,
And the beard of his chin was as white as the snow.

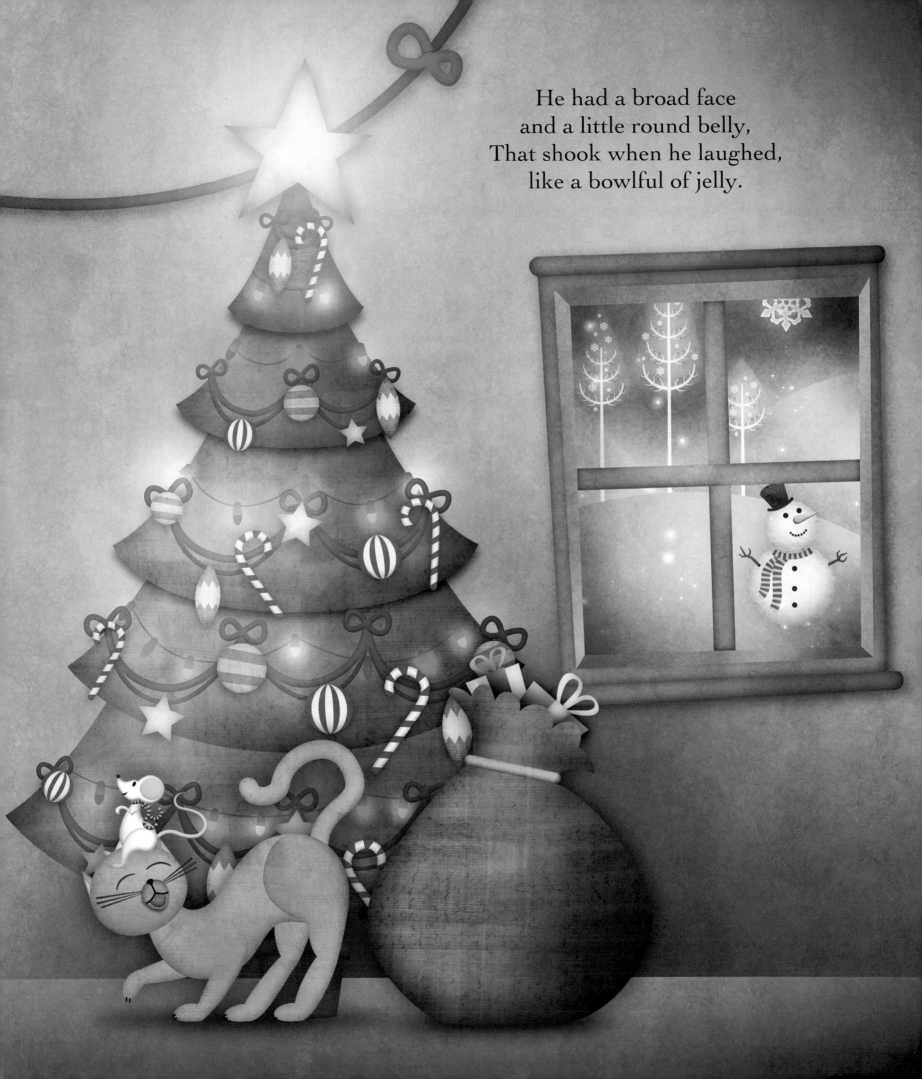

He had a broad face
and a little round belly,
That shook when he laughed,
like a bowlful of jelly.

He was chubby and plump, a right jolly old elf,
And I laughed when I saw him, in spite of myself.
A wink of his eye and a twist of his head,
Soon gave me to know I had nothing to dread.

He spoke not a word, but went straight to his work,
And filled all the stockings, then turned with a jerk,

And laying his finger aside of his nose
And giving a nod, up the chimney he rose.

He sprang to his sleigh, to his team gave a whistle,
And away they all flew like the down of a thistle.
But I heard him exclaim ere he drove out of sight,
"Merry Christmas to all, and to all a goodnight!"